MY DOG MADE ME WRITE THIS BOOK

ELIZABETH FENSHAM

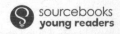

sourcebooks
young readers

Published by Sourcebooks Young Readers, an imprint of Sourcebooks Kids
P.O. Box 4410, Naperville, Illinois 60567-4410
(630) 961-3900
sourcebookskids.com

Originally published as *My Dog Doesn't Like Me* in 2014 in Australia by
University of Queensland Press.

Names: Fensham, Elizabeth, author.
Title: My dog made me write this book / Elizabeth Fensham.
Other titles: My dog doesn't like me
Description: Naperville, Illinois : Sourcebooks Jabberwocky, [2019] |
   "Originally published as My Dog Doesn't Like Me in 2014 in Australia by
   University of Queensland Press." | Summary: Ugly, the dog, prefers
   everyone in the family to eight-year-old Eric, his owner, but when Eric's
   crazy ideas fail to win over Ugly, he tries something more basic.
Identifiers: LCCN 2018057204 | (trade pbk. : alk. paper)
Subjects: | CYAC: Human-animal relationships--Fiction. |
   Dogs--Training--Fiction. | Family life--Fiction.
Classification: LCC PZ7.F3484 My 2019 | DDC [Fic]--dc23 LC record available
at https://lccn.loc.gov/2018057204

Source of Production: Berryville Graphics, Berryville, Virginia, USA
Date of Production: May 2019
Run Number: 5015025

Printed and bound in the United States of America.
BVG 10 9 8 7 6 5 4 3 2 1

To the readers of this book, including the children
who want their dogs to like them.

And in memory of our beloved family dogs:
Lassie, Laddie, Simon, Shane, Jason, Maud, and Toby.
-E.F.

For Ash the Schnauzer:
We will never forget you or your doggy farts.
-J.L.

1

Running away is a very difficult thing to do if you are going to do it right. To be warm and safe, there's a lot to organize. Before I knew it, my school backpack was almost full, and I had packed only a book, my coat, and a chocolate bar. I still needed to take:

- a blanket
- a flashlight
- a water bottle
- some sensible, healthy food
- my whistle
- two extra books to read in case I never saw a library again in my whole life

- some paper and a pen
- my tin of pocket money

How was I going to carry all that?

In the end, I snuck out to Dad's shed and grabbed the wheelbarrow. When Mom was in the bathroom, I crept into the kitchen and raided the pantry and fridge. I put on my backpack and dragged the rest of my stuff out to the wheelbarrow.

ECCLE'S RUNAWAY ESSENTIALS

SENSIBLE + HEALTHY SNACKS

BOOKS

BLANKET

PEN + PAPER

MY WHISTLE

WATER BOTTLE

FLASHLIGHT

POCKET MONEY

Unfortunately, my horrible big sister, Gretchen, spotted me. She laughed in a tease-y way and said, "I'll help you run away, Eccle! Here, give me that." She tried to take the wheelbarrow from me, but it tipped over. Everything fell out. Then she stooped down to put all my things back in.

"Better give us your new address," said Gretchen in a nasty, cheerful voice.

I didn't answer. I started pushing the barrow up the driveway and along the sidewalk. I was heading for the little park two doors down. Our neighbor, Mrs. Manchester, was drinking a cup of tea on her front porch. Her ginger cat, Penelope, was draped over her lap like a rug. "Off for an exciting adventure, Eric?" she called out to me.

How was I supposed to reply to that? Mrs. Manchester must have thought I was like a three-year-old playing make-believe. As I turned to reply to the old lady, I noticed Gretchen had followed behind like a spy. She called out to Mrs. Manchester, "Eccle is running away from home!"

"Oh dear me," said Mrs. Manchester. "Your parents will be very worried."

I didn't wait to hear more. In a fury, I put my head down and pushed that wheelbarrow so hard and fast that I was trotting like a pony. Gretchen's cruel tongue gave me a spurt of energy. When I got to the playground, I stopped and sat on a bench. I was panting, and my heart was thumping—out of anger and sadness.

Ugly had brought me to this. I was homeless because of a dog. Tonight, he'd be safe and warm. Maybe he'd take over my bedroom. Where would I be? I might even be in danger. That scared me—stranger danger. How would I stay safe?

I looked around. It was a summer evening. The sun was sinking lower and lower in the sky. Spooky fingers of shadow were sliding across the grass toward me. In the sunshine, I felt I could cope. But what would I do in the dark? Was I going to stay on the bench all night, or find somewhere else? By now, Gretchen the spy had turned and gone home. No one cared. I was alone in the world.

I started to realize that running away was very boring. I sat and sat on that hard, wooden bench for a whole half hour. I ate my chocolate bar. Then, a mom with a baby in a stroller and a noisy little boy walked into the park. The mom looked tired; she sat on another bench and texted someone on a cell phone while her noisy boy played around on the swings, the slide, and the other play equipment.

•••

After the mom and kids left, a beat-up-looking car stopped and three teenagers got out. They played on the equipment too, and were just as loud as the little boy had been. No one spoke to me, but I didn't mind. I didn't want anyone asking questions. I pretended to read my book, but I was too upset to concentrate. That shows how sad I was, because I usually love reading.

After that, it got almost dark. I started imagining all the things that could happen to me. In the middle of my imagining, I noticed a creepy-looking man. He had a cap pulled down over his eyes, and he wore a black, baggy coat. He was hanging around the edge of the park.

Sometimes, he'd walk out of sight. Then, he'd come back again. My heart started thumping in my chest; it was going in all directions like a terrified wild bird trapped in a room. What a stupid, dangerous thing I was doing—being all by myself.

People's backyard fences were left, right, and behind me. Should I climb one of them and ask for help? What if I climbed into someone's place and they thought I was a robber? What if the people were bad guys? I was stuck. How I wished I were safely at home reading a good book in my bedroom. Reading an adventure about a boy running away is much more fun than actually running away, I realized.

I reached down and picked up a heavy stick to protect myself from the scary man. Next, I took my whistle out of the wheelbarrow and got ready to blow it loudly. But then I noticed the man's bent back and the way he shuffled and limped a little.

It was Grandpa! He was keeping an eye on me.

Someone cared.

That's when I decided to go home—but not with Grandpa. That would be giving in to the rest of the family and Ugly, who didn't care. I stood up and rearranged my things in the wheelbarrow, trying to look busy. Grandpa shuffled farther down the street toward home. I quietly followed, keeping a distance.

● ● ●

After Grandpa went inside the house, I waited a few moments. Leaving most of my things in the wheelbarrow, I slipped through the open front door. I crept down the hallway. Second door on the right, and I was back inside my bedroom. I sat on my bed, enjoying feeling safe and warm, until Dad appeared and invited me to the kitchen for a family chat.

Most of what was said can wait for later, but in the end, I was sent back to my room for being rude to Gretchen. Now, I wouldn't mind being sent to my room if I'd been rude to Mom or Dad or Grandpa, but Gretchen? It's like the victim is in prison and the bad guy is free. Boy, was I mad.

I was stuck in my room for so long (actually, for the rest of the night). At first, I was too upset to do anything—not playing games or even reading, which I really love. That left me with nothing much to look at except for the curtains Mom had made me with the dog pictures all over them, which made me even sadder. The curtains reminded me of my eighth birthday more than a year ago.

It was while I was stuck in my room feeling all clogged up with miserableness that I became an author. I thought I might start writing down my sad and angry story. It's been over a week now since I became an author. After I finish writing each part, it feels good to get everything off my chest.

2

My dog doesn't like me. It's a fact. When I got back from running away, I explained this to my family.

"Hogwash," Grandpa grumbled, and he stomped out of the kitchen and down the back steps to his veggie garden.

My big sister, Gretchen, muttered, "You are such a loser," and kept on filing her fingernails.

Dad said, "What a bunch of nonsense!" He walked away and sat at his computer to do his bills.

Mom bent down, patted the dog, and said, "Poor guy."

The dog looked deep into Mom's eyes, as he always does. He knows how to get her on his side. But I'm telling you the truth. My dog truly, truly doesn't like me. He won't give me the time of day. I'm not sure what "time of day" even means, but I know he wouldn't give it to me. I just don't exist for him.

I know because that silly dog just won't spend any time with me. He loves Mom; he follows her around like a bad smell. Grandpa says that about Gretchen's boyfriend, Shane. It exactly describes my dog, Ugly. For one thing, if Mom stands up, he gets up off the floor. If Mom walks to one room, he plods after her. I swear, if Mom twirled and whirled in little circles, Ugly would turn in circles too.

And as for "like a bad smell," that's my dog all over—especially when it's been raining and his fur is wet and spongy like sheep's wool. Mom is what you call a "neat freak" and likes things clean and tidy, but Ugly is allowed to plod through the house and leave his big, round doggy footprints on the floor. And if I did that? I'd get yelled at.

I said that to Mom as an example of how she's made Ugly her favorite.

She said, "Don't be silly. *You* know better. And you can take your shoes off or wipe your feet, but a dog can't."

"He can too," I said. "If he is as intelligent as you think he is, then he could learn to wipe his paws."

Before Mom could admit I might be right, Gretchen said, "You're jealous, Eccle!"

"Am not," I said.

Gretchen laughed in a nasty way and said, "My little brother is jealous of a dog!"

I could feel the tears prickling my eyes, but I didn't

want Gretchen to see. "I'm not little. I'm older than nine now. And I'm not jealous, and you're the sister of a dog." I didn't get time to explain, because Dad was already angrily pointing me toward my room.

"I don't want to hear you talk like that again, Eric!" he said.

I only get called by my full name, Eric, when someone's angry with me. (Eccle or Ec is what I called myself when I was two years old because I couldn't pronounce *Eric*.) So this time, I knew Dad was really angry.

"That's the second time in just a few hours that you've been unacceptably rude," said Dad. "First to your mother, and now to your sister. It stops now!"

As I've already explained, I was totally miserable stuck there in my bedroom. Tears were leaking from my eyes, although I was trying to stop them. Until the moment I decided to start writing a book, I even thought about running away again. No one takes me seriously.

• • •

Even as I was being marched out of the kitchen, I noticed that Ugly—who was lying with his snout across Mom's feet as she sat at the table—lifted his head and twitched one ear for only a moment. Then he dropped his head back onto Mom's shoes, as if to say, "Is that what the fuss is about? Just that kid being difficult again?"

I'm not jealous of my dog. I'm just disappointed in him, and I have good reason. Actually, I'm not just disappointed in him. If he doesn't like me, then I don't like him either!

3

When I said my dog doesn't like me, you might not have noticed that important little word "my." Ugly is supposed to be *mine*. He was my present for my eighth birthday.

●●●

I had always wanted a dog. Mom and Dad decided it was a good idea for me to have one for a few reasons. Firstly, having a big, bossy sister who is ten years older than me means I can sometimes feel a little lonely. And although no one said it to me, I think my family felt I needed to get out and exercise more.

"With big feet like yours, you'll eventually grow into them," Grandpa says, but the rest of my family says I'm "on the chubby side." Walking a dog seems to be one way people stay in shape. But all of the walks Ugly and I take are disastrous. He pulls really hard on his leash, dragging me along so that my feet nearly fly off the ground.

But back to my birthday. Turning eight felt good. I've always liked the shape of an eight—like a racetrack. And the idea of a dog for my present seemed fantastic. In the Bright family, we have a birthday breakfast. You have whatever your favorite food is, and you get to open your presents after that. I had pancakes, berries, and ice cream, and then I ripped into my gifts. They all had a dog theme.

●●●

First were Mom and Dad's presents. Mom had sewn me some new bedroom curtains and a cushion cover made with amazing material that had pictures of different dog breeds all over it. Dad gave me a red tartan dog collar with a matching red leash, plus a padded dog bed with raised sides to keep out uncomfortable breezes.

Grandpa gave me two bowls (one for water and the other for food) and a book called *Lassie*, which is about a really faithful, clever dog.

Gretchen gave me a bag of dog biscuits and heart-worm medication. She said, "You could also benefit from some deworming medication, Eccle."

I felt hurt. Gretchen rolled her eyes and said, "Just joking!"—words she often throws at me after she says something mean.

Mom said, "Ease up, Gretchen. It's your brother's birthday."

Gretchen's mouth went the shape of a squashed strawberry. She leaned back in her chair and crossed her arms. Because it was my birthday and because I was now eight years old, I tried to be grown-up, so I shrugged and smiled. But I know that it's unfair to say mean things and then pretend it was a joke.

Anyway, after Gretchen's "joke," Dad got us all talking about what sort of dog I could choose and where we'd find one. We all agreed that the dog should be medium-sized. We'd get him or her from the dog shelter, which is an orphanage for dogs. I liked the idea of rescuing an unwanted orphan.

I took the dog collar and leash to school to show the class.

Travis Petropoulos said, "Those are weird birthday presents." But most of the kids were happy and excited for me.

My birthday ended really well. I came home from school with the two friends I'd been allowed to invite—Hugh Cravenforth and my ex-fiancée, Millicent Dunn. (Milly and I were engaged for a week in our first year of school, but that got boring. She wanted flowers and a ring—all that sort of stuff. Now we're just good friends.) Mom had arrived home early from work and had baked me a cake in the shape of a smiling dog with its tail sticking happily up in the air.

Before we dug into cake and ice cream and "wore it all over our faces," as Grandpa called it, Mom took a photo of us. It's now sitting in a frame on my dresser. I'm standing in the middle between my friends. My hair

~ MILLY, ME, AND HUGH ~
: AT MY 8th BIRTHDAY! :

is wet and freshly combed, but straw-colored pieces are already sticking out. I can see I had more of a tummy back then. Hugh is on my left. He has dark, curly hair, and he's tall and bony—big knees and elbows. Milly is on my other side. She has her light-brown hair pulled back in a ponytail with a big blue ribbon. She has the friendliest smile, with a wide gap between her two front teeth.

After the birthday cake, Grandpa invited us down to the backyard to help him build a dog kennel. The kennel was a real surprise. Grandpa had bought all of the wood and nails. There was even a plan he had torn out of a weekly magazine. Grandpa said we'd build a big kennel so it could fit just about any size of dog. Being good with handwriting, Hugh painted a little sign to go over the doorway—DOGHOUSE. Milly and I held the wood together while Grandpa sawed and nailed. He did a great job, considering he'd had a hip replacement only three months earlier.

● ● ●

Building that kennel was one of the best times I've ever spent with my grandfather. He isn't a talkative man. In fact, he sounds a little grumpy even when he's being nice. If someone is unlucky enough to call our house and Grandpa answers the phone, he has a strange way of saying a member of our family isn't home.

For example, if someone asks to speak to Dad, he'll more than likely say, "No. He went to Timbuktu and hasn't been seen since." There'll be silence at the other end of the phone.

But when Grandpa was working with us on the kennel, he asked us questions about school and our teachers, and he even told us about his school days way out in the country, "Where the crows fly backward to keep the dust out of their eyes." At Grandpa's country school, all five grades were in one classroom. And even more amazing was how the kids in elementary school all over Australia were given teeny-weeny glass bottles of milk the size of a small jam jar for lunch so that they would grow up with strong bones. The milk was free from the government. By the time it was getting dark, the kennel was half built, which was good progress. Then Dad got home, Mom called us in for spaghetti (my favorite dinner), and Gretchen got off the internet in time to eat with us.

During dinner, Dad announced we were going to the dog shelter the next day. I was over the moon. I was going to get my doggy birthday present.

All of the Bright family went to the animal shelter with me, but I was the one who was going to make the final choice. It was one of the best but saddest days of my life—both at once. There was cage after cage of lost, unwanted, or abandoned dogs. I wished I could give them all a home.

You wouldn't believe how many different kinds of dogs there were. Mom has a funny book she's kept since she was a kid where you flip half a page over and create new dogs from the front of one page and the back of another. A lot of the dogs looked like they'd come out of Mom's book—as if some scientist had played around with them. Some were smooth, some hairy. Spotty, silky, curly, and scruffy. Brown, black, blonde. Some had floppy ears, some had pointy ears. Beady eyes or big owl eyes. Some long noses, some little noses. Some were as small as your hand, and others were as big as a small horse. Some were fully grown, and some were puppies. And the noise! Barking, howling, sniffling, whimpering, yapping, and yowling. It's like most of the dogs knew that when visitors came, it was their chance to have a home. They were calling for attention.

• • •

Each of us had our favorites. Mom fell in love with a cute spaniel with one leg missing. Dad liked a young Kelpie cross, but he said working dog breeds need a lot of room to run around. Gretchen went nuts over a tiny dog with bulging eyes; I swear it was the size of a rat. Grandpa didn't say much, but he spent a lot of time patting a big old German shepherd who was so skinny you could see her ribs.

How was I supposed to choose? Luckily, it wasn't going to be up to me. I got chosen.

I had stopped to look at three fat puppies with shaggy bangs hanging over their eyes and wiry sandy-brown hair on their bodies. One was curled up by itself in a corner. The other two were play fighting. The bigger one was winning. She was a girl. She was a rough player—always knocking her little brother off his feet and pouncing on him. But he was great at wriggling out from under her. Then he'd jump on his sister, but she'd

BIG
BULLY
☠ SISTER ☠
(JUST LIKE GRETCHEN)

POOR LITTLE UGLY
(JUST LIKE ME)

throw him down in a sort of karate hold. He'd squirm and nip. She'd lose her grip a moment, he'd escape, and then it would begin all over again.

That sister is just like Gretchen, I thought. *And her little brother has the same sort of messy, straw-colored hair as me. He's also tough, just like I want to be...*

"Never say die," said Grandpa quietly over my shoulder.

"What does that mean?" I asked.

"Never, ever give in," said Grandpa. He patted my shoulder and walked on to join Mom, Dad, and Gretchen at another cage.

I laughed. I knew what it was like to be the little brother who could never stay on top for long. The shaggy little brother must have heard me. He walked away from his game with his sister and trotted over to me. His bright, intelligent eyes looked at me from under his bangs. And I swear he was smiling with his neat little needle teeth.

He jumped up against the wire and looked straight into my eyes. His big sister wasn't going to let him speak to anyone else. She bounded up behind him, jumped on his back, and latched onto the loose skin around his neck. But the little brother shook off his sister—and he kept looking at me.

"This one!" I called over my shoulder to Mom, Dad, Gretchen, and Grandpa.

Gretchen was the first to walk across to me. "That?" said Gretchen.

"Yep," I said.

"It's as ugly as sin!"

Gretchen's words helped me make up my mind even more.

"He's the one I want," I said. "And I'll call him Ugly."

5

Maybe my dog hates being called Ugly. Maybe that's why he doesn't like me. But I don't think it's that. The day I picked him, he said "thank you" by licking me all over the face. Anyway, if he doesn't like his name, he gets plenty of variations. Sometimes he's Uggie or Ug or Ug-Dog or Ug-Paws. Like me, Ugly looks like he's growing into his paws. He's over a year old and still growing.

It might seem silly to get this upset about a dog, but for so long I'd had this dream of what owning a dog would be like. I pictured myself walking along with him, my hand resting on his back. He would keep to my side like a loyal companion. He'd be waiting for me at the door when I came home. He'd fetch things and do tricks and come when I called. He'd sleep on the floor at the end of my bed and guard me all night long. He'd be my best friend.

•••

But instead, Ugly is Mom's best friend.

It hurts.

He doesn't obey me. I'm not even on his list as second-best friend. There's Grandpa, then Dad, then even Gretchen comes before me—and she's just as bossy with the dog as she is with me. So nothing adds up. Ugly has been a disappointing birthday present. It's as if Mom got the present, not me.

And Ugly does mean things. He pounces on me and bites my ankles. A few weeks ago, he got into my room and pulled my ancient Greece project off my desk. I'd made the famous temple, the Parthenon, out of hundreds of matchsticks. Ugly chewed them all up. The carpet was covered in tiny pieces of wood like straw. On top of that, I've had enough of being yelled at for not properly controlling or doing my share of work for Ugly.

On the day I ran away, the whole family was on my back.

"Have you fed the dog? You keep forgetting."

"Ugly just pulled Mom's apple cake off the kitchen table."

"There's no water in Ugly's bowl."

"Ugly's digging a hole under the fence into Grandpa's veggie garden."

"Ugly's stolen Gretchen's undies and torn them to pieces."

"Ugly's had an accident on the kitchen floor. Get a bucket of water and a cloth and wipe it up."

"Ugly's chewed on one of Dad's antique chess pieces and another one's missing."

"Ugly's dragging Gretchen's tights around the backyard."

"When was the last time you took Ugly for a walk?"

●●●

Well, just to answer that question: on that horrible day that I was sent to my room, the last time I'd taken Ugly for a walk was an hour before I ran away. And what did he do on that walk? He took off after another dog. He pulled me along on his leash until I tripped and gashed my knee on a stone. I lost hold of the leash and nearly killed myself trying to get across the road to grab him. Then I had to pull him away from a fight with a nasty, big, black dog. Ugly thought it was really funny. His tail was wagging hard. When his tail hit my legs, it hurt. I yelled at Ugly.

The black dog's owner, a tall man with a dark beard, told me I shouldn't yell at a dog and that I needed to have more control over him.

"Whose dog is it?" asked the owner.

"Mine," I said.

"Well, you should know better."

But is Ugly mine? I get told off by everyone about him, but he's really Mom's dog.

I tried to explain this to Mom by using a phrase we had learned in class. She went ballistic. She didn't like what I said, even if I *had* been taught it by our teacher. Just the other day, Miss Jolly taught us all these famous sayings like *crocodile tears*, which means pretend tears, and *snake in the grass*, which means someone who's sneaky. Miss Jolly calls them *idioms*. An idiom is understood in your own language, but if you tried to say the

same thing in another language (like Japanese or Italian, for example) people would be very confused. Maybe if you spoke to someone in Italian and told them they were a snake in the grass, they'd stare at you and say, "I am not a snake. There's no grass here. I'm a human standing in my kitchen!"

There's one idiom I especially remembered. It's *barking up the wrong tree*. It's when you're looking in the wrong place…or accusing the wrong person.

●●●

When I got home from that last walk, all bloody and scratched from rescuing Ugly, I'd told Mom what had happened and what the black dog's owner had said.

"Well, there's some truth in his words," said Mom. "You don't do enough for Ugly.

You've been pretty lazy."

WAG
WAG WAG

ARFF!
ARFF! GRRR
ARFF!

There it was again. Blame me.

So I said to Mom, "You're barking up the wrong tree. You stole my dog. He's your dog now, and you're both hopeless."

Boy, did that start something. Mom looked red in the face like a volcano about to spew lava. She started shouting things like, "In my day, they'd have washed your mouth out with soap and water," and, "You're being a lazy lump!"

So Mom thought I was a lazy lump. Now I knew for sure. Mom didn't love me.

"You love that stupid dog more than me!" I yelled back. "You're a bad mother!"

"How dare you!" cried Mom. I escaped to my bedroom before she could yell anything else at me, and that was when I started packing my things to run away.

6

When I was little, I liked the fairy tales Mom would read me. It's interesting how the number three often comes into stories like that. There's the two ugly stepsisters and Cinderella (three sisters in total), the three little pigs, the three brothers in *Puss in Boots*, and it always seems like people are given three wishes for something. So this gave me the idea that I should give Ugly three chances.

Chance number one is that I'm going to call Ugly something different, just in case he hates his name. Maybe he will be nicer to me if I change his name. His new name has to sound like "Ugly" because it would be confusing for someone to call you something really different. For example, if I didn't want to be Eccle or Eric, maybe someone could call me Rick. Rick is the last sound on my name—Eric. I might do some research. I'll ask my family first.

• • •

This morning I did my research, and now here is my list:

- Umberto—Grandpa says he used to work at the jam factory with a lovely Italian man named Umberto. He would sing opera while he glued the labels onto jam jars.
- Ulysses—Dad came up with this name. Ulysses was a hero in an ancient Greek legend about the Trojan War.
- Ualtar—Mom is into reading about anything to do with Ireland. She gave me this Irish name, which means "strong fighter."

- Utterly—Gretchen said my research was "utterly peculiar," so, take it or leave it, "Utterly" is my suggestion for you.

Mom's name—Ualtar—is too difficult to pronounce. It's sort of like Walter, but the "U" sound is different than the "U" in Ugly. The same goes for Ulysses. It'd be really good to name my dog after such a noble hero, and Ugly might be stoked too, if I could explain. But there's still the problem that the "U" sound in Ulysses is like the "oo" in "zoo." No, Ugly needs to be able to recognize his name.

●●●

The best names have come from Grandpa and Gretchen. Their suggestions have the same starting sound as "Ugly"; the "U" sounds like someone who's huffing and puffing up a hill with his mouth wide open. I have already tried the names on Ugly. It's hard to know if the experiment is working. You see, as long as I have a treat like a dog biscuit in my hand, Ugly will come to either name.

"Here, Umberto!" Up runs Ugly and snatches the biscuit.

"Here, Utterly!" Up Ugly runs again and almost takes my finger with the biscuit.

Then I try "Ugly!" and he comes just as quickly.

After that, I thought I'd test my experiment. I decided to call Ugly something totally different— "Pamela!" (which is Mom's middle name)—and still he came.

But when I tried calling Ugly any of those names without offering a biscuit, he just settled himself down under the kitchen table and ignored me. I crouched down and came right up to his face. His messy bangs were hanging over his eyes, like one of those high school rebels the teacher tells to "Get a comb and clean yourself up!"

I said to Ugly, "Come *now*!"

Ugly opened one eye and squeezed the other shut.

I've seen TV detectives do that squeezy thing with their eyes when they're suspicious.

"Come on, boy! Come, Ugly! Umberto! Ualtar! Ulysses! Utterly! Pamela!" I pretended to run for the door.

Ugly gave a sort of bored groan and dropped his head onto his paws.

Ugly has failed the test. He has tossed aside a chance to prove himself to me. He has also shown himself to be selfish and to have bad manners. Dad is always saying we should be grateful for the kindness people show us and we shouldn't use and abuse their friendship.

There's another idiom that our teacher, Miss Jolly, taught us—*cupboard love*. It means you show love to someone only because they will feed and look after you. It exactly describes Ugly. He is a cupboard lover and a user. I think that someone who will only be your friend if they get some sort of reward is a weak and nasty person.

Ugly is darn lucky I'm a man who sticks to his word. A weaker person would throw out Ugly's two last chances when he discovered what I have. A few minutes ago, I smelled something horrible in my bedroom. I started looking around. Was it a dead mouse? Some cup of cocoa I'd left somewhere that was growing mold? A pair of socks I'd worn for a week and left under a pile of clothes?

No.

Any and all of those things would be better than what I've just found. I was looking in my closet, on my desk, behind my chair. Then I just lifted up my bedcover and looked under my bed.

There it was.

A pile of dog poop, still steamy and warm. Ugly has insulted me.

7

As I've been saying, Ugly should be grateful he's even got two more chances, especially after the mountain of stinky poop he secretly left under my bed.

When I woke up this morning, I didn't have a clue what sort of second chance I'd give Ugly. I got up and decided to eat breakfast first. My brain needed good ideas, and I can't think well on an empty stomach. To get to the kitchen, I had to walk through the family room. Gretchen was lying on the sofa and painting her fingernails a candy-pink color with sparkles.

"So has Ugly been friendlier when you call him Utterly?" she asked.

"Don't tease. You know he couldn't care less what I call him. He ignores me no matter what."

"Maybe even dogs can sense a weirdo when they meet one," she said, spreading her fingers out to inspect her nails.

"You're…you're…" I couldn't find anything equally nasty to say back to my sister.

"Let me finish your sentence for you, Ec. I think you were going to say to me, *You're right, big sister. I'm weird*," said Gretchen, blowing on the wet nails of one outstretched hand. "Now I'm going to be kind and give you a word of advice. You need to do some real research about dogs, not just ask around the family."

● ● ●

During lunchtime at school, I told Hugh and Milly all about my unhappy time with Ugly. Until then, I'd kept pretty quiet about what was going on at home. I'm not sure why; maybe partly because I didn't even understand why having Ugly had turned into such a flop, and maybe partly because Hugh and Milly had worked hard to build Ugly's kennel and make him feel welcome, and I didn't want them to be disappointed.

"Gretchen says I need to do some real dog research. I thought I could find out from kids at school how they would handle Ugly," I finished.

"Excellent idea!" said Hugh, his dark eyes shining. Milly flicked her ponytail the way she does when she gets excited. "Lucky we did that research project on *Health and Leisure* last semester," she said. "We now know how to make a questionnaire."

Milly got a clipboard, paper, and a pen from the classroom, and then the three of us sat down in the shade of our favorite pepper tree to brainstorm. In the end, we decided to do a public survey, like they do at the big shopping centers where people walk up to you and ask questions and then write down your answers.

Milly said that to get the best ideas we needed to

ask at least ten people, and they had to come from a range of different grades. Hugh said we needed only one question, and he told us to ask it like this:

Pretend you have a dog (even if you don't) who doesn't like you; what would you do to get your dog to like you?

Hugh neatly printed our question at the top of the page. Then we set the rest of the page out with Name, Grade, Age, and Answer sections. We took turns asking and writing. We got all the research done in one lunch hour:

Miles Bucknell. Grade One. Seven years old:
  "I'd throw the dog a bone. In fact, I'd throw it a
  lot of bones."
Emily Wright. Grade One. Seven years old:
  "Let it smell my hand. Be gentle so it'll think I'm
  nice and friendly."
Merri Spalding. Grade Two. Eight years old.
  "Get it another puppy to play with."

Eden Hogg. Grade Five. Eleven years old:

"I'd play with her."

Liam Smith. Grade Four. Ten years old:

"I'd pet her and spend more time with her."

Callum England. Grade Two. Eight years old:

"I'd buy her some dog toys."

Angus Fletcher. Grade One. Seven years old:

"Walk him on a leash."

Poppy Giles-Kaye. Grade Four. Nine years old:

"Give it treats."

Skye Denbigh. Grade One. Seven years old:

"Throw him a ball and tickle and scratch his tummy."

Alara Güleçoglu-Park. Grade Six. Twelve years old:

"I'd hypnotize the dog."

Aiden Starbuck. Grade Three. Eight years old:

"Make a dog club so he has some friends."

William Segala. Grade Six. Eleven years old:

"Put on your mother's clothes and put on a wig
that looks like your mom's hair and even

45

wear her perfume so your dog thinks it's her."

Tilly de Lacy. Grade Five. Eleven years old:

"Get a goldfish instead."

Sarah Gloor. Grade Five. Eleven years old:

"Dress him up to make him popular."

Oliver Barlass. Grade Six. Twelve years old:

"The owner should dress up like a juicy dog bone."

Travis Petropoulos. Grade Six. Twelve years old:

"Dogs like milk. Give him milk."

Cornelius Chang. Grade Six. Eleven years old:

"Never shout or call him bad names, but sing to him."

The bell rang just as we'd written down Cornelius's answer.

"We'll meet under our tree tomorrow at lunchtime," said Hugh as we lined up outside class.

"We need to analyze the data," I said.

"Data?" asked Hugh.

"The data is all the information we've gathered," explained Milly. "And sorting through it and discussing it is analyzing."

"You're on," said Hugh.

By the time I climbed into bed, I felt a lot happier. Sharing my problems with Hugh and Milly was a sensible thing to do.

I couldn't wait to get to school today. Milly, Hugh, and I analyzed yesterday's research. Hugh had a clever way of sorting through the kids' answers.

"First off, we should get rid of ideas that you've tried and that haven't worked," said Hugh.

"Yes, it's a good idea to eliminate them," I said, "but I can tell you now, I'm pretty sure I've tried every sensible idea to get a dog to like you that a person can think of. For starters, you can cross off dressing a dog up."

"Don't worry about that," said Milly. "There'll still be some leftover ideas you can try out."

Hugh, Milly, and I were back under our pepper tree.

Milly pointed to Angus Fletcher's idea about walking the dog.

"I've tried that, but Ugly just about rips my arm off." Milly took a red pen and slashed a line through Angus's dog-walking idea.

"What about Aiden's idea about a dog club, or Merri's idea about getting another puppy? Maybe Ugly is lonely," said Hugh.

"No way. At the moment I couldn't control Ugly if he was in a dog club, and Mom wouldn't stand us

49

having another dog. Anyway, Ugly would probably just be friends with the puppy and like me even less."

Milly slashed two red lines across the page. "Well, what about bone throwing?" asked Hugh.

"Give Miles's idea a check mark," I said. "I haven't tried bones yet."

"That's pretty much the same idea Poppy had when she talked about treats and Travis's idea about milk," said Hugh.

"Yeah, it is," I agreed. "But a good bone is an enormous, delicious treat—sort of like Christmas dinner."

"Then again, giving treats is a type of bribing," said Milly, "and my dad says people should do the right thing without having to be bribed."

"Ugly isn't a person. He's a dog," I said. "If bribes work, I'll be glad."

Milly gave a big red check mark to bone throwing.

"Well, next is Emily's idea about letting the dog smell your hand and acting gentle around it."

I knew all about that. Grandpa had told me before we went to the dog shelter. "That's the right thing to do when you meet any dog," I said, "but after that first introduction, you have to live with your dog every day of its life. The same goes for Skye's idea. Ugly likes being tickled and scratched, but you can't keep doing that all day."

Milly crossed off Emily's and Skye's ideas. "Dog toys?" asked Hugh.

"Ugly's a spoiled brat," I said. "He's got tons of toys, but he gets bored with them and sneaks off and chews up things that belong to us, like my Parthenon project."

"Dressing yourself up as a dog bone?" asked Milly.

"You'd have to be bonkers," I said. "A dog might eat you! And cross off the idea about dressing in Mom's clothes. No way."

"What about singing to a dog?" asked Hugh.

"He doesn't seem to like singing. He barks viciously when Gretchen plays her heavy metal CDs, and he howls like he's at a funeral when Mom plays her opera CDs," I said.

"Okay," said Hugh, "then we can bundle up some of these other ideas, like throwing a ball and playing and spending time with him."

"Is he like a neglected child?" asked Milly. "Just wanting more attention from you?"

I thought about the times I had tried to play ball with Ugly but he had run off with the ball and chewed it to pieces. "I'm the neglected one," I said.

"I'll put a red line through the ideas about playing and spending time with him," said Milly, "but I really think you could try harder at playing."

"Well, the bone-throwing will be a type of playing," I said. "A game with food. You can't go wrong. It's got to be a big hit with Ugly."

9

It seemed a stroke of luck that when I walked into the house that afternoon, I had the place to myself. Mom, Dad, and Gretchen were still at work, and Grandpa was snoring away on his bed. Even Ugly was sharing Grandpa's afternoon sleep. He was lying on his side in a pool of sunlight next to Grandpa's bed. When he saw me out of one squinty eye, he thumped his tail on the floor, shut his eye, and went on sleeping. I opened the fridge door to see what I could raid.

There was some freshly-squeezed orange juice and leftover pasta from last night's dinner, which I hungrily scarfed down. I decided to give the contents of the fridge one more inspection. What should I find at the bottom but a big leg of lamb covered with a tea towel! Mom was obviously going to roast it tonight.

I thought of the research Hugh, Milly, and I had discussed. Underneath all that meat there was a huge bone. My family wouldn't be needing it. All I had to do was cut off the meat so Mom could cook that—and here was a bone for me to throw to Ugly.

It was hard work slicing off the meat from the lamb bone, but I got off as much as I could. I neatly laid the meat on a plate and put it back in the fridge with the tea towel over it. Then I quietly returned to the living room and waved the bone at Ugly, who had opened one eye again. He scrambled to his feet and followed me to the kitchen. His eyes gleamed, and he was grinning and thumping his tail against the table.

Without even having to speak, I walked out the back door and down the steps with Ugly following close by me. On the lawn, I held the bone high above my head and told Ugly to sit. I didn't even have to push his butt down. He sat right away and woofed.

I threw the bone with as much strength as I could. It flew over the kennel and across to the far side of the backyard. Ugly took off after it, quickly reaching it and pouncing on it like a lion attacking its prey.

"Okay. Come, Ugly. Bring it back here!" I called.

What a fool I'd been. Why had I expected Ugly to come back with a meaty bone when he wouldn't even come back with a tennis ball?

I yelled and stamped my foot, but he just picked up his bone and hid behind Grandpa's toolshed, up next to Mrs. Manchester's fence.

I was so angry that I left Ugly in the yard and stomped back up to the kitchen. But I wasn't as angry as Mom was when she came home from work and went to take the roast out of the fridge to put it in the oven. I tried to explain that we didn't need the lamb bone, but Mom couldn't see my point. Dad,

Gretchen, and Grandpa couldn't, either. I have to agree that those pieces of meat on the plate didn't look like very much. I'd left more meat on Ugly's bone than I realized.

Mom decided to make shepherd's pie with the leftover slices of lamb and a lot of chopped vegetables. Gretchen stared into the baking dish and said, "There's not enough meat in there for two people, let alone five. Eccle should have bread and water, like a convict."

"We'll make do," Mom said in a grumpy voice.

"You're too soft on that boy. You were never like that with me. At least make him eat an egg," Gretchen whined.

"Give me an egg, then," I said. "See if I care."

"Okay, you asked for it," said Mom.

Mom had just put the casserole dish in the oven when we heard a long, loud yell from the back garden. Grandpa had gone out to water his vegetables, but we could hear him marching up the steps. He burst into the kitchen.

"Eric!" he bellowed. "Your dog has dug a gigantic

hole in my carrot bed! If your mother ever wanted her lamb bone back, it's now buried."

Before I could finish saying sorry, Grandpa said, "And that's not all! You'd better get out there and give the dog a good wash."

"What's happened?" asked Dad.

"As well as destroying my carrots, he's gotten into the compost pile, eaten those old fish heads we threw out the other day, and rolled in all that dirt as well."

"Out you go, Eric, and don't come back till that dog

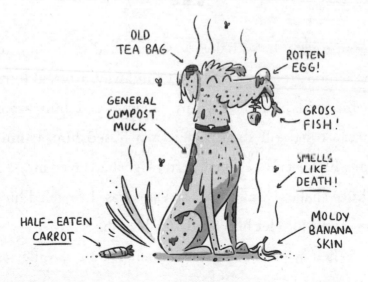

OLD TEA BAG

ROTTEN EGG!

GENERAL COMPOST MUCK

GROSS FISH!

SMELLS LIKE DEATH!

HALF-EATEN CARROT

MOLDY BANANA SKIN

smells as sweet as a newborn baby," ordered Dad. I'm not so sure a newborn baby smells sweet, but I wasn't about to argue with Dad. By the time I was in the back garden with Ugly's leash, a bucket, dog shampoo, and a towel, Ugly had escaped under the house. Grandpa's yells must have sent him hiding.

I had to commando crawl under the house, attach Ugly's leash to his collar, and drag him out. He smelled like something that had been dead for a year.

● ● ●

Because Ugly hates being washed, I had to tie him to the lemon tree so he couldn't run away. I hosed him, shampooed him, hosed him, shampooed him again (because he still stank), and then hosed him a third time. By the end, especially after Ugly had given himself a huge shake, I was as wet as Ugly was. I toweled him dry, and Mom let him inside for his dinner.

When we sat down for dinner, I kept as quiet as

possible. Ugly lay under the table, his nose resting on Mom's feet and his butt up near my feet. Nothing had changed. He'd been happy to take a huge lamb bone from me, bury it in Grandpa's carrot patch, eat compost and roll in it, and then watch me get into trouble. Mom was still the one he loved.

I was just dipping my toast into my boiled egg when Gretchen, who was sitting next to me, made a face and said, "Eccle, you smell disgusting!"

"Does he?" asked Mom.

"He's farted," said Gretchen.

"I have not!"

"Phew," said Dad, swatting at the air in front of his nose. "Something's powerful in here."

"Own up, Eccle. I know a fart when I smell one," said Gretchen, leaning away from me.

"Something's rotten in the state of Denmark." Grandpa got up to open a window.

By now, I could smell it too. I've been to the local

garbage dump with Dad and Grandpa, and here, in this room, was a thick and putrid smell that reminded me of the garbage dump in a heat wave.

"It's you, Eccle!" said Gretchen again. "You should be ashamed of yourself."

"Abandon ship!" called Grandpa. He grabbed his dinner plate and left the room. Mom, Dad, and Gretchen did the same.

"It's Eccle's very own chemical warfare," said Gretchen as she slammed the door shut.

I stayed behind, staring at my boiled egg in its eggcup. After a few moments, a fresh wave of stink swept around me. I lifted the tablecloth. The stink poured up at me. It was coming straight from Ugly's butt. You can't eat old fish heads and other rotting food and get away with it.

I can't say Ugly farted on purpose, but it's just another example of how I get blamed for everything Ugly does. I'm seriously wondering if I should tell my family to give Ugly away.

10

"The compost and fish heads would have definitely made the farting worse," said Milly.

It was lunchtime the next day. Hugh, Milly, and I were under our pepper tree again. I'd been telling them about the night before and what Gretchen now called the "Emergency Evacuation."

"How come fish heads make it worse?" asked Hugh.

"A completely meat diet added to stinky fish heads and old food scraps makes the foulest stink in the universe," said Milly.

"I wonder if a vegetarian fart would smell better?" I said.

"Probably," said Milly. "My uncle is a vegetarian. He says meat takes longer to digest. It rots in your body."

"Anyway, the bone-throwing method is now definitely ruled out," I said.

Milly crossed bone-throwing off our list. "Okay, don't give up hope, Ec. We've still got hypnosis."

"Hypnosis is where you put someone to sleep and then talk them into believing what you want, right?" I asked.

"Something like that," said Milly.

"It's all about controlling the mind," said Hugh. "I heard my big sister talking about it. The most successful people on Earth have mind control over themselves and other people."

"And dogs?" I asked.

"Why not?" said Hugh.

"How do you control a dog's mind?" I asked.

"Same as with a person. You get them relaxed and concentrating, and then you make positive suggestions to them," said Hugh. "Deep, deep down, the person is listening and believing. Like you might say to someone who's a smoker, *Your lungs are black and disgusting and you'll probably die by coughing up blood, so you'd better give up smoking and start exercising,* and then they go and do what you say. With Ugly, you'd probably say, *Obey me. Obey me. I'm your lord and master.*"

"But how exactly do you relax the person and make her concentrate?"

"Well, a well-known way is to use a man's pocket watch. Do you know what that is?"

I did know. Grandpa had inherited his dad's pocket watch. He kept it on his bedside table. On special occasions, he would let me hold it. It was the size of a large, round sink plug, made out of shiny silver with fancy patterns carved into it. A long, silver chain was attached to the little knob on the top. If you wanted to know the time, you just pressed the little knob and the shiny front would click open. Under the cover was

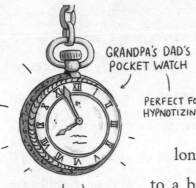

GRANDPA'S DAD'S
POCKET WATCH

PERFECT FOR
HYPNOTIZING?

a clock. In the olden days, a man kept his watch in his waist-coat pocket, and the long chain would be attached to a button so he didn't lose his precious watch.

I loved being allowed to touch my great-grandfather's pocket watch, but it didn't make sense how such an old-fashioned thing would be used to hypnotize someone.

"Do you make someone listen to the ticking?" asked Milly.

"No," said Hugh. "You hold the chain and swing the watch sideways, back and forth, back and forth, in front of the person's face. You tell them to concentrate and you speak to them really calmly. You just do the same thing to Ugly. Easy as pie."

"Why is pie easy?" Milly asked.

"Darned if know," replied Hugh.

"I think it might be an idiom," I said. "It probably means that eating a pie is easy. But I'm not so sure that hypnotizing a dog will be as easy as you think."

11

Step one to hypnotizing Ugly was getting Grandpa's permission to use his watch for a while. It turned out to be surprisingly easy. I was allowed to play with it for half an hour on the condition that I didn't take it out of the house.

Next, I had to get Ugly into my bedroom. I couldn't risk distractions like people barging in and out of a room. When I managed to get Ugly in there, I closed the door so he couldn't escape.

I thought the third step of my plan was clever. I put on calming music, but with no singing. It was a CD that Mom used for relaxation, one with sea and wind sounds to harp and flute music. I also gave Ugly some dog biscuits. I thought that if I needed food to think, Ugly probably needed food to concentrate too. After that, I gave Ugly a brush-down with a grooming brush. He liked that, except for the part on his tummy, near his back legs. When I brushed there, his back legs started moving. I think he was ticklish.

As anyone can see, I did my best to make Ugly feel at home in my room.

When Ugly was lying on my mat beside my bed, looking relaxed, I crouched down and spoke to him.

BEHOLD THE ENCHANTING

ECCLE

TOTALLY UNINTERESTED

"Ugly," I said, "You must watch what I do." Ugly looked at me.

I held the pocket watch by the chain and started swinging it slowly back and forth. "You will love and obey me. You will love and obey me," I started to say. Ugly liked this. For a moment, he was really interested. His ears pricked up straight. His eyes looked bright. He smiled. But then he did something silly.

He snapped at the watch! He was trying to bite it.

I held the watch farther from his face. Ugly thought this was fun.

He thumped his tail on the floor, gave a happy bark, and threw himself at the watch again. Luckily, it swung away from his mouth.

"This is not a game, Ugly," I said. "Get serious." I clipped his leash onto his collar and tied the other end to the doorknob, so Ugly couldn't jump at the watch again. I pushed down on Ugly's butt to make him sit. Then I started all over again. Back and forth with the pocket watch.

It looked like Ugly had got the idea. His ears were up straight again, and he watched the clock swing. His shaggy head tilted left and right. He was grinning and panting.

"Love and obey me. Love and obey me," I said.

Ugly yapped. Then he leaped so hard at the watch that he yanked the leash and fell backward. Even that didn't stop him. He got up and went for the watch again.

"You idiot!" I screamed. I threw myself on the bed and jammed my face into the pillow. Tears leaked out of my eyes without permission.

Ugly was barking away. He sounded glad that I was upset.

I heard a knock on my door.

"What's going on in there?" It was Grandpa's voice. "Can I come in?"

"Okay."

Grandpa opened the door halfway.

Ugly swung around and started pawing Grandpa's legs.

"Why's your dog tied to the door handle?"

"He's not my dog. He doesn't want to be."

"Well, what are you doing mistreating the poor dog?" asked Grandpa. He immediately untied Ugly, who escaped out of my room.

What a traitor that dog was. "Trying to hypnotize him."

"What would a silly fool like you want to do that for?"

"To make him like me." I sat up on my bed.

Grandpa spotted his pocket watch still clutched in my hand. "And you were using my father's watch to do this?"

"You know about using a watch?"

"Of course I do," said Grandpa. "But even if that sort of thing works, in your situation, your chances are slim to none."

I guessed Grandpa was using an idiom here, but I was too upset to ask for it to be explained. I just knew Grandpa meant I had no hope of hypnotizing Ugly.

"No use?" I asked.

"The first thing you need to know about hypnosis is that the subject has to want to do the thing you're suggesting."

"Subject?"

"The person—or dog—you're hypnotizing. They'll only agree to do what they want to do."

"So because Ugly wasn't interested in being hypnotized, it means...he...doesn't...want...to...be...my... friend," I said, between little gulps. It felt like my heart was crying. It was going all the way up my throat.

● ● ●

Grandpa did something he doesn't often do. He sat down on my bed and gave me a hug. He smelled of mown grass and sweaty armpits. The prickly white stubble on his chin scratched my forehead, but I liked the way he crushed me to his bony chest.

"It's not too late. Your dog can still be your friend. You just have to be his leader."

"But how? I've been trying!"

I didn't know what Grandpa meant. I really had been trying. And I'd failed.

"I said *leader*, not *dictator*."

"What's the difference?"

"A good leader is kind."

I still felt a little confused, but one thing was clear: my grandfather was hugging me because I was sad and lonely, and he wished I wasn't. That was good enough.

12

I n a lot of made-up stories that I've read, the problems seem to get solved really quickly. In a make-believe story, I would have woken up the next morning and somehow Ugly would instantly look up to me as his leader. But that's not real life.

What happened was this: I woke up the next day feeling calm. I knew I wasn't all alone in trying to get Ugly to like me. Grandpa understood my problem, so I'd ask him to help me.

It was a Sunday morning, a few days back. I had dressed quickly and then gone to have breakfast. Ugly was under the kitchen table. As I walked in, he thumped his tail in a welcoming sort of way.

"Morning, Ugly," I said. As I bent down to give him a pat, I realized he had probably said hello to me many times before, but I was in the habit of only noticing what Ugly did wrong. Maybe I should take more notice of when Ugly did things right. But for the moment, I needed to concentrate on figuring out how to be his leader. After eating my porridge, which Grandpa makes for the family every morning, I went out into the backyard to look for Grandpa. He was tidying up his tools in the shed. "Hey, Grandpa," I said, "can you tell me more about how to be Ugly's leader?"

"Sure thing. You can help me hang these tools on the shadow board. We'll talk as we work."

I started to pass Grandpa tools as he asked for them. He hung them on hooks on a pegboard he'd built on the wall.

"First off," said Grandpa, "if you're the one who

looks after your dog, he will naturally see you as the important one. Looking after means feeding, grooming, walking, playing, and training."

"I already do some of that," I started to say.

"Listen up," said Grandpa. "It's the same old story for a lot of youngsters. It's the mom who does most of the hard work."

"So?"

"So, unless Ugly sees you doing most of the work, this talk of ours is going to be pointless. Pass that hammer, please."

To be honest, the word "work" sounded boring. Having to do jobs, even stuff like learning multiplication, at a certain time every single day isn't my thing. Moms are good at it, not kids.

"I've got school and all that. I'm pretty busy," I said.

Grandpa was just standing there, staring at me with his eyes all big. He snorted in an annoyed way and pointed at the door. "If you're busy, what does that make your poor, overworked mom? Out you go! You're wasting my time."

That scared me. I really wanted Grandpa's help. I realized I was skating on thin ice.

I held my hands up, like people do in films when a gun is pointed at them. "Kidding! I'm listening, Grandpa. Just tell me what I need to do."

"For starters, you should write up a timetable. You'll have to ask your mom what sort of chores she does for Ugly. When you've done that, come back and we'll talk some more."

●●●

I found Mom. She was giving Ugly's grooming brush and comb a wash in the laundry bucket. I wrote down everything she said. I already knew most of it, but making the list made me take notice. What she did for Ugly made me feel bad. This is my list of Mom's chores:

And all of this was before and after she went to work. Saying I had school was a weak excuse.

Next, I started on my timetable. Trying to fit in the morning jobs meant I had to wake up earlier. Then, I added the evening jobs, and realized I'd have to cut back on my free time if I was going to get everything done. I read my new timetable and sensed something was missing. What had Grandpa said you had to do for a dog? Then I remembered. It was feeding, grooming, walking, playing, and training. I looked at the incredibly long list of things Mom did for Ugly. She fed, groomed, walked, and watched Ugly's health. But I was right— two things *were* still missing. They were things Mom had not had enough time to do: train Ugly effectively and play with him. I felt a light bulb go off in my head. I knew why Ugly had chewed up my Parthenon project. He was bored.

13

"ow do you make a dog unbored?" I asked Grandpa at breakfast the next morning.

Mom and Dad had already left for work, although Gretchen was rushing through the kitchen to get her car keys off the wall hook. She heard what I said and joined in.

"Try having a personality change, Ec. That might help."

"Very funny. Ha, ha," I said in a deadpan voice. I surprised myself by speaking this way. It was better than sulking. For once, Gretchen didn't have a nasty comeback.

"It's actually an interesting question," said Grandpa,

taking a gulp of hot black tea and a bite of marmalade toast. "And, Eric, you've put your finger on one of the keys to encouraging a dog to willingly obey you."

"Likely!" said Gretchen, throwing her keys in her handbag.

"Your words exactly, Gretchen," said Grandpa. "More than likely—a certainty. Naturally, all dogs love playing, but an intelligent dog like Ugly also enjoys learning and communicating. In a nutshell, if someone plays with and trains Ugly, he will not be bored."

Gretchen tossed her head in a snooty way. "Well, bored dogs are low on my list. I have more import-ant things to do, like get to work and talk to human beings." She rushed out of the room.

Grandpa said we'd talk more at the end of the day after school. "Now, put your timetable under one of those magnets on the fridge, and get that dog fed. You do your part, and I'll spend the day thinking about what Ugly and you need to do."

It was comforting knowing that a grown-up cared enough about my problems to spend a day thinking about them.

At school, when I told Hugh and Milly about what Grandpa was saying, they both agreed I was lucky to have a grandfather to give me advice.

None of Hugh's grandfathers were alive. "But I have a lovely grandma. She taught me to knit," he said.

"Grandparents can teach you useful things." All four of Milly's grandparents lived in other states. "We chat online," said Milly. "I sometimes play a word game called Scrabble with one of my grandfathers."

"Yes," I said, "grandparents are special. I wonder what Grandpa will say makes a dog unbored?"

"Spending time with your dog," said Hugh. "It was somewhere on that list when we did the research. I'm always wanting my dad to spend time with me."

"Me too," said Milly. "Dads seem to be at work a lot."

"And moms too," I said. "They seem tired and

worried a lot of the time; that's why grandparents are good. They're too old to go to work, but not too old to spend time with you."

When I got home after school, Grandpa handed me a fruit juice and a muffin. "As soon as you've had your afternoon snack, you need to read your timetable and start working on your dog chores."

"What about your ideas for making Ugly unbored?" I asked.

"Don't worry. I haven't forgotten. My first idea is that if you're the one feeding and exercising Ugly, he'll be easier for you to train. Easier to train means he won't be bored. First things first: What does your timetable say?"

I looked at the timetable on the fridge:

After school—four o'clock: Feed Ugly. Groom Ugly. Walk Ugly.

"Boring," I said. I folded my arms on the kitchen table and dropped my head on them. "I'm tired. It's been a long day at school. Even longer than usual."

"That makes no sense," said Grandpa. "How can a school day be longer?"

Oh dear. I'd said too much. I tried to get Grandpa offtrack. "Nice muffin," I said. "Did you make it?"

"You know I'm the muffin king around here. Stop stalling. Why was your day long?"

"I was kept in at recess. Unfairly."

"How so?"

"Because I failed my multiplication test."

"Why did you fail?"

"No time to practice."

"Why no time?"

"I'm too busy." I waved my hand at Ugly's care timetable stuck on the fridge.

"Busy!" said Grandpa. He didn't actually *say* it. He snorted like a horse. "Now listen up: Training a dog. Doing schoolwork. Learning multiplication. Being a sports star. Playing a musical instrument. It's the same thing. Discipline and routine. You start looking after your dog adequately, every day—even when it's boring, even when you're tired and don't feel like it, even when there's something better to do. Then we'll talk."

Talk about cranky. How come I thought Grandpa was the nicest one in my family?

So I fed Ugly. Then, I made him lie on his mat while I combed him and gathered up all the clumps of hair and put them in the garbage. Then, I walked him.

14

The walk wasn't any better than usual. It was a drag. That's a pun. There are two meanings for *drag*, see? "Drag," meaning "really, really boring," and "drag" as in "pull." Ugly tugged on his leash and pulled me along. His nose would find an interesting smell and he'd drag me around: back, forth, left, right, and around in circles. Worst of all, on our way back from the park, Ugly met Penelope, the ginger cat who lives next door at Mrs. Manchester's. She was sunbathing on Mrs. Manchester's low brick fence. For the billionth time on one of our walks, I lost control of Ugly.

Ugly flew after the cat. I hung onto his leash. If I

could draw well (which I can't), I'd have Ugly moving like one of those Japanese bullet trains and me in the air behind him, clutching his leash—wind pushing the hair back off my face and my legs flying straight out behind me like a flag in a storm.

I expected Penelope to run away, but she stayed put. She had attitude. Her back went into a spiky arch the shape of Sydney Harbour Bridge. She spat, snarled, and clawed at Ugly's face. Ugly put his tail between his legs and backed off for a moment. Then, his tail started wagging. He turned his head to the side and raised his little brown eyebrows up and down, as if he wanted to ask the cat a question. The cat hunched low. Ugly was smiling, and then he started yapping. He was glad the cat was standing up to him.

I thought Ugly might want a playmate. But I instantly changed my mind. Ugly growled and pulled his lips back in a nasty, wolfish

PENELOPE, THE TRAUMATIZED CAT!

way. He leaped at the cat, who shot up into the air as if she had been thrown straight upward. Penelope did this amazing midair twist, and the next minute she was off, tearing toward her house. Ugly tried to jump the brick fence to follow the cat, but I hung on with all my strength.

By the time we got home, my right arm was nearly pulled out of its socket. Ugly trotted along beside me, pretending he didn't know I was upset. I call that emotional bullying. We learned about that in school. It is when you mean to hurt someone's feelings and then you make it even worse by ignoring the person, like Ugly was doing.

If Ugly could talk, he would have said, "I was just having fun. What's the problem?"

AHHHHHHHHH

ME, THE
"TOTALLY IN CONTROL"
DOG OWNER
(NOT!)

UGLY, THE RUNAWAY
BULLET TRAIN!

I knew he'd say that, so I answered him out loud, "You're a bully. I'm telling."

●●●

What did Grandpa say when he heard all this? "It'll get better. Stick to it."

But things got worse. The phone rang. I heard Grandpa saying, "Sorry... Yes... Of course. I'll make sure it doesn't happen again..."

After putting the phone down, Grandpa turned to me. "That's old Mrs. Manchester. She's very upset about her cat being traumatized by your dog. I don't want to hear a complaint from her again."

So once again, it's "your dog" when Ugly does something wrong.

I don't like Ugly, and I don't like my grandfather.

15

This is Ugly's last chance, of course. It's a long-last chance. Hugh and Milly say I should stick to what Grandpa has told me to do, so I've been trying. I've been doing most of the feeding and some of grooming and walking. I promised Grandpa I'd do this for two whole weeks, and I've mostly kept my promise, but I'm a little forgetful. My family doesn't seem to appreciate the effort I'm making.

Dad says "forgetful" is an excuse for "don't want to." Mom says, "Parents can't pick and choose when they'll look after their children. It should be the same with you and your dog." Gretchen usually says something to my parents like, "I keep telling you he's spoiled."

There have been some improvements with Ugly—slower than a snail, mind you. He now knows it's me who mostly does the feeding. A few times when he's wanted his dinner, he's found me wherever I am and nudged me with his nose, or he's sat next to where I'm sitting and stuck his paw on my knee, staring hard at me with those big brown eyes of his. I think he's trying to hypnotize *me* now.

The best thing is that Ugly now greets me when I get home from school. He can hear me as soon as I come in the front door. He runs up to me, barking, smiling, and hitting me with his tail.

I'm also becoming more alert to Ugly's naughty tricks. The other day I prevented a crime Ugly almost committed. I was doing my math homework at my bedroom desk when out of the corner of my eye I saw a dark shadow moving very slowly—almost gliding like a shark does. It was Ugly, creeping toward the door with something in his mouth. I slowly turned my head a little more. Ugly had one of my sneakers in his mouth. He didn't know I could see him. What amazed me was his sneakiness. Ugly knew he was being a thief. He knew he shouldn't be stealing my things, but he had it all planned out. Just before he got to the door, he started to speed up.

"Stop!" I said firmly.

Ugly flopped down on the floor. He still had the

sneaker in his mouth, but he had a guilty expression. He didn't want to look me in the face. I walked up and took the sneaker away. Normally, Ugly would want to make a game of this and hold on tight—but not this time. He let go of my sneaker and then he slunk away. This shows that Ugly is starting to see me as his master.

Ugly's failed shoe robbery got me thinking. Ugly is clever. He thinks things through. He plans stuff. He knew he needed to move slowly so that I didn't notice, and then he timed it so he knew when to make a dash for freedom. When he was caught red-handed (or in Ugly's case, red-mouthed), he looked guilty and embarrassed, just like I'd be. If I was Ugly's schoolteacher, I'd say what Miss Jolly said about me in my midyear report:

"Ugly has some challenges with completing learning tasks at home. Nevertheless, he has enormous potential if he can be more disciplined."

I liked the word "potential." I looked it up after I got my report from Miss Jolly. It means *a possibility or likelihood of becoming something in the future.* So on this thirteenth day of October, I can see that Ugly does have potential. It is possible for him to learn to obey me, but I'm stuck as to how to go further.

Walks are still horrible. Ugly pretends to be good until he sees something he wants to chase. My arms are getting stronger from hanging onto the leash, but I can think of better ways to build my muscles. How do I cure a dog who thinks he's a hunter?

Most nights, after his walk, Ugly lies in his usual spot under the kitchen table. He falls asleep on his side, his legs making running movements and with little *woof* sounds coming out of his mouth. Even in his dreams, Ugly is chasing enemies.

●●●

While I was in the middle of writing my book tonight, Grandpa popped his head around the door. "Get back quickly from school tomorrow, okay?"

"Okay," I said. "Grandpa, do you realize that Ugly only has two days left of his third chance?"

"I do indeed," he said.

So now I'm sitting up in bed, writing away. I don't feel sleepy at all. Firstly, I want to know what Grandpa has up his sleeve. Secondly, and much more importantly, I want Ugly to pass his third test, but I can't see how I can do any more for him. Although Ugly is still annoying, I'm starting to like my dog.

16

When I got home today, I banged through the front screen door, patted Ugly who had come to meet me, and then walked up the hall, through the family room, and into the kitchen. That's where I'll often find Grandpa in the afternoon. He'll have finished his odd jobs and veggie gardening, and he'll be sipping a cup of tea. And that was where I found Grandpa, but someone else was there with their back turned to me. I couldn't see the face because the person was wearing a wide, battered straw hat.

"There you are," said Grandpa as if he'd been looking for me and I was late. "I have a surprise visitor for you."

The stranger swung around and stood up—a tall woman wearing baggy pants and a flannel shirt with the sleeves rolled to her elbows. She looked younger than Grandpa, but not by a lot. Her hair was short and gray above a round face that was smooth and brown with rosy spots on each cheek; she was the only person I've ever met who had what Mom calls "apple cheeks."

"This'd be Eric, then," said the woman, her blue eyes crinkling up as she smiled. She stepped up to me and held out her hand. I put my hand forward, and she gave me such a strong handshake that I had to hold my breath to keep from saying "ouch."

"Having some dog trouble, are we?" she asked.

Who was this woman? Why had Grandpa been telling her my business?

I mumbled something like, "Maybe."

Ugly was excited that we had a visitor and excited that I was home from school. He danced around for a minute and then jumped up on me.

"Down!" said the big woman when Ugly jumped up. She was standing next to me, but she held her hand in front of Ugly's face like a traffic policewoman and stepped close to him—what Gretchen would describe as invading Ugly's personal space.

"Sit!" said the lady in a strong, low voice. Ugly stepped back and sat.

"Good boy. Good, Ugly," said the lady, patting his head and slipping him what looked like a small piece of a dog biscuit.

MAGGIE:
THE AMAZING
DOG WHISPERER

WHISPER

UGLY:
THE OBEDIENT
ANGEL
WHAT?!

97

"Meet Maggie Buchan," said Grandpa. "She's my old school friend Charlie Buchan's younger sister, and she's over from Western Australia to visit her granddaughter for a few weeks."

"Oh," I said, wondering what the big deal was.

"Maggie trains dogs," Grandpa added.

"And dog owners," said Maggie in a stern voice.

"She's never failed," said Grandpa. "Maggie's my present to you. Concentrate and learn all you can about dog training."

"I hear today's Ugly's last chance," said Maggie.

Hearing about my troubles from a stranger was embarrassing. What would she think of all this stuff about me giving Ugly three chances? From an outsider's view, I might look kind of awful. Giving a dog a last chance? It seemed mean.

I stared down at my feet. "I guess."

"Nothing more frustrating and unpleasant than a disobedient dog," said Maggie in a kind way.

She understood! I looked at her to check if she was kidding. "And a dog that didn't like me until just recently," I said.

"Ah, yes," said Maggie. "But you'll have to face something, Eric."

"Face what?" I asked.

"*You* are the main part of the problem."

"Me?"

"Yes, face the facts, Ec," added Grandpa.

How harsh can you get? Me? The problem? How dare she! Someone—okay, a dog—has shown for weeks that he couldn't care less about me, and *I'm* to blame? And *face the facts*? What a tough thing for Grandpa to say.

But I'm not a wuss. I've suffered great hardship: been forced to run away, had my Parthenon model chewed up, found stinky poop under my bed, been dragged into life-threatening situations on dog walks, been ignored, and been laughed at. A person can only take so much. Maggie is just a bigger, older version of Gretchen.

Did I tell that to Maggie? No way. But she must have seen my face.

"Stormy weather today?" she said, peering at me.

I think I might have inherited Gretchen's cranky-strawberry-mouth look. You can't talk well when your mouth is the shape of a squashed strawberry.

"Dunno what'cha mean," I mumbled. I knew I was being rude to a visitor. I wouldn't have blamed Grandpa for giving me a stern look, but he didn't do that.

He just said, "It's your last chance, Ec. Listen up to Maggie, or you're done for."

Heck no. Everyone was getting it wrong. It was Ugly's last chance. When would grown-ups get it right? And I said that. "It's Ugly's last chance, not mine."

Then came the shock of my life. I'm still shaky as I write this down.

Grandpa said, "Well, Eccle, it's actually both of

your last chances. You see, your mom is tired—she's worn out with the long hours she has to do at work. She was telling me last night that although you have improved your work ethic, she still can't give Ugly what he needs. Gretchen's no help. Your dad is also overextended at work. That leaves you and me. And you know that since my hip operation I just can't do what I used to do. The poor dog is neglected, and he's getting out of control. He's growing bigger than we expected—a risk, I suppose, when we didn't get to see his parents—and big dogs need a lot of exercise and plenty of discipline."

"But I've nearly always stuck to the timetable," I said.

"Not as often as you trick yourself into believing," said Grandpa. "Your mom is tired of finding half-filled cans of dog food lying around the kitchen benches, dog biscuits scattered on the floor, Ugly's water bowl empty, or precious belongings chewed to pieces because Ugly is still getting bored from not enough exercise."

"I'm not that bad," I said. I held my breath, waiting for what he was going to say next. But at the same time, I sort of guessed. My heart was pounding. My hands were sweaty.

Grandpa continued, "If things don't change, your mom, dad, and I are thinking that Ugly might be better off with a family who knows something about looking after and training big dogs."

"No!" I yelled. "You can't make Ugly an orphan. You can't just kick him out. And I've been trying to help. You know I have, Grandpa."

17

I felt sick. I had to fight for Ugly's right to stay in our home. I truly didn't know how I was going to save my dog. I felt like someone who was drowning because they were trying to rescue someone else who was drowning—hopeless.

After I had begged Grandpa not to make Ugly an orphan, he took a while to reply. I guess he was choosing his words carefully.

"You've certainly tried a little harder to pull your weight with the feeding and walking and all that, Ec. But it's not so simple. This is a small house. It's a squeeze fitting five humans into it, let alone a growing dog into the bargain."

Pleading hadn't worked with Grandpa. What shocked me was that he was for real. He really had been discussing Ugly's fate with Mom and Dad. The three of them had made big decisions about Ugly and me without my permission. I couldn't help it; my voice started wobbling uncontrollably.

"No, Grandpa, no! I beg you! You can't do this."

Ugly must have understood something. He started getting worked up. He was jumping around and barking. His tail hit a cardboard box of Grandpa's tomatoes that was sitting on a small side table. Tumble went the box. Sprawl went the tomatoes. Jump, jump, twirl went Ugly. *Squish*, *splat* went the tomatoes. It looked like blood and guts all over the kitchen floor.

"See for yourself," said Grandpa, waving his hand around at the mess. "The proof is in the pudding. My best tomatoes of the season. Gone!"

Oh, cut out these idioms, I thought. *Yes, Grandpa, your precious tomatoes are destroyed, but you can't say*

THE
TERRIBLE TOMATO
DISASTER !!!

Ugly's accident proved what you're saying is right. This mess wasn't Ugly's fault! It's...it's everyone's fault. This last part I said in a blurt, except I changed it a little:

"It's not Ugly's fault!" I yelled. "It's yours. And Mom and Dad's. And Gretchen's!"

"Calm down now!" said Grandpa in a loud voice. "You're blaming everyone but yourself. If you keep doing that, you'll never grow up. Show some character, Ec. Like I've said before: own up to it!"

Ugly got really worked up and started jumping on Grandpa. Maggie took Ugly by the collar and put him outside through the back door.

She held her hands up, open-palmed toward Grandpa and me, like the policewoman she must have once been; she looked as if she was in charge of crowd control at an NFL match. "Not in front of the dog, thank you. Set him an example."

Grandpa and I were both panting as if we'd just run a race. I should have been worried about Grandpa having a heart attack, but I wasn't thinking about that. I was actually thinking that maybe Ugly and I should run away—and do it right this time. We have to stick together. It's amazing how many thoughts can zoom through your brain in a few seconds. Next thought was that we couldn't run away because I knew I didn't have enough money to feed Ugly. I had to think smart. Think clever. How do you do that?

For one, you don't make your grandfather any angrier.

"Sit down, Grandpa," I said. "I'm sorry about the tomatoes. I'm sorry about saying nasty things about my family. I'll clean up the mess."

Grandpa plunked down in his chair, leaned his elbows on the table, and put his head in his hands. He was still getting his breath. It came to me then that all this chaos isn't good for an old man. This fight could kill him. I'd be a murderer.

"Good boy," said Maggie. She figured out where the kettle was and started getting Grandpa a cup of tea while I went to get the compost bin and a rag, as well as the mop, and began the disgusting job of cleaning the floor.

While I was working, Grandpa, his head still in his hands, said quietly, "We're not trying to be cruel to you, Ec. It's just that it's all too much."

I didn't trust myself to say a lot. I had to save Ugly from a terrible fate. I had to control myself. "Sure, Grandpa. What do I have to do?"

"Over to you, Maggie," said Grandpa.

We all sat down at the table. I put my extra-polite, listening-carefully face on. Maggie explained that she was going to come three times a week for a few weeks to show me how to train a dog. Actually, the words she used were, "to train you how to teach your dog."

●●●

The deal is I have to keep up Ugly's lessons before and after school, as well as on weekends. Maggie will give me a test just before she goes back home. If I pass this test of hers, I get to keep Ugly, and the two of us will go to puppy school for a few months at the local vet's.

Of course I said "yes" to everything. And I do think it's a good thing to learn how to train your dog. I also agreed that I'm lucky to have an expert give me some lessons for free. But I really don't agree about the "or else Ugly goes" part. That's totally unfair.

I didn't say that, though. I said, "Thank you, Maggie, I'll try my hardest."

Maggie said the first lesson would start tomorrow after school. Then she said she had to go. I was happy about that, because I was finding it hard to look cheerful. After Grandpa and I waved Maggie goodbye, I took Ugly to the park. I sat on the swing, and Ugly sat opposite me and plunked his paw on my leg. He knew I was feeling down.

"Thank you, Ugly," I said. "I have to tell you some terrible news. They're sending you away if I can't train you right. We have to stick together, or we're done for."

Ugly turned his head to the side, like old people who have bad hearing do when they want to use their good ear for listening carefully. That's what Ugly does when he's concentrating. His bright eyes looked straight at me from under his messy bangs. I know he understood because something amazing happened later.

I was sitting up in bed, reading my latest library

book. I'd pushed the bedroom door nearly shut. I like to be private, but I also like to hear what's going on around the house. At around eight thirty at night, something shoved at the door, and it moved a little.

Was Gretchen spying? No.

The door swung open a little farther and Ugly walked in. He trotted up to my bed, looked at me, and then jumped right up. I put my arms around him and we snuggled. I was almost asleep when I wondered what Mom would think about a dog on my bed. I got out, went to the family room, and brought back Ugly's dog bed, which I put at the foot of my own bed. I gave Ugly a hug and then gently moved him off my bed and pointed to his bed. Ugly climbed on. I got back into my own bed and went to sleep. In the morning, when I saw Ugly still asleep in my room, I couldn't believe it. It was what I had dreamed of and hoped for when I first got a dog. Ugly definitely likes me, but is it all too late?

18

At recess today, I told Milly and Hugh all about my troubles and how I was going to have my first dog training lesson this afternoon.

Later during the day, Miss Jolly was stern with me because I was being fidgety.

Milly told Miss Jolly, "Eccle is facing an ordeal when he gets home."

"He's in deep trouble," added Hugh.

Miss Jolly came over to me while the other kids were doing small group work. "Would you like to speak to me about this ordeal, Ec? It sounds like you have to go through something painful and dangerous."

"No one can help, really," I said. "It's all up to me."

"Is this something scary and bad? You're not alone if you share a problem with a grown-up you can trust. A problem shared is a problem halved. Maybe I could help you?"

"If you are an expert at dog training it might help," I said.

"Oh dear," said Miss Jolly. "I only have a cat. They tend to train the humans. Anyway, I'm sure everything will turn out okay."

Miss Jolly meant well. I knew she was checking to see if I was safe at home. But her saying she was "sure everything will turn out okay" was just washing her hands of the problem. "Washing hands" is another idiom, but there's too much on my mind to research this one.

Milly was more helpful. Just before the bell rang, while we packed up our belongings, she said, "Write down everything the dog lady tells you. Stick the list on the wall next to your bed so you can revise."

Maggie was waiting for me when I got home. She'd brought a dog harness for Ugly.

"This makes it easier to control a dog when it's on the leash," she said.

Ugly, Maggie, and I went outside to the backyard for our first lesson. It was about heel, sit, stand, come, and watch me.

Ugly seemed to like his lessons most of the time, especially as Maggie told me to pat him, tell him he was a good dog, and then give him treats every time he got something right. He seemed to learn faster that way. A few times, he got bored and misbehaved, but then, Maggie told me to play a game with him. I'd throw Ugly's ball or play tug-of-war with his rope, and then he'd concentrate again.

Maggie has a clever way of teaching a dog to heel. You just go a few steps and then reward the dog. Then, you make him go a little farther and reward him again. Maybe I'll be able to walk Ugly without having my arm yanked off. I also liked the way Maggie used hand movements with voice commands. She didn't even have to speak; she just used the hand movements to tell Ugly what to do. I can think of tons of times it'd be useful not to have to speak aloud when you're with your dog.

● ● ●

The dog training—or should I say "dog-owner training"—was interesting. But like waves dumping on a beach, I kept remembering that if I didn't become a good trainer, I would lose Ugly.

I think Ugly understood how important it was to behave. His ears were sort of half down, in a sad kind of way. He kept looking at me all through the training session, as if to say, "I'm trying my best. Do you think we're winning? They're not going to send me back to the orphanage, are they?"

Knowing the lesson was serious helped me concentrate, but it's not a nice way to learn. Even tonight, as

I'm writing this in my bedroom, I keep looking at Ugly and my heart turns over. He's a lovely dog.

I asked Maggie for the dog training rules, and I scribbled them out using my own words. This is a neat copy here:

1. Don't drag out the training; keep the lessons short and interesting (just like school should be).

2. Swap lessons around in a different order each time so that the dog doesn't start guessing what's going to happen (which means it's more interesting).

3. Start off using yummy treats as rewards. When your dog gets the hang of his lesson, only sometimes give a treat.

4. Give your dog tons of praise when he obeys you, but don't make a big deal when he messes up. You want a happy obedient dog, not a scared obedient dog.

5. Don't get mad at your dog for getting things wrong.

6. Never, ever scare your dog.

7. Don't physically punish or hurt a dog.

8. You should be patient and kind during every training session. Never shout—that's just a human's way of barking.

9. End a training session happily. Finish with something your dog does well and praise him a ton, and maybe reward him with a treat. He'll then think that training sessions are fun and look forward to the next one.

10. A good way to make training fun and never boring is to
break it up with playing and walks.

"Good to see you taking this seriously," said Maggie
as I was writing.

"I want to keep Ugly," I said.

"We'll see how you're doing by the time I have to
go back home," said Maggie. "He could be a handful if
he's not adequately trained soon. He's an active little
fellow, and he's still growing. Imagine if your grandfather got knocked over and broke his other hip! You'll
really need to be consistent with Ugly."

I asked her what "consistent" meant.

"Regular," said Maggie.

So that's why I'm confused and sad tonight. Maggie
could see I was trying today. And I know I'll keep my
promise about being regular with Ugly's training, but that's
just not good enough for the grown-ups around here.

19

I was training Ugly on my own today, which was hard without Maggie being there. Ugly likes his treats, but if I were his schoolteacher, I'd write in his school report that he should try a little harder. Miss Jolly doesn't feed me every time I get a multiplication question right. And what's really annoying is that Ugly doesn't remember yesterday's lessons.

The training session was even harder because halfway through, Gretchen came and sat on the back steps and watched me. It felt like she was just waiting to see Ugly or me get it wrong. And that's what happened.

While I was trying to get Ugly to walk at heel, he dived under my legs and I fell splat on the grass.

"That could have been Grandpa taking a tumble," said Gretchen in her know-it-all voice. "The grown-ups are right. That dog should probably go."

"Ugly just got badly distracted and scared," I said.

"By what?" asked Gretchen.

"By seeing your face," I said.

I grabbed Ugly's leash and we ran around the side of the house before Gretchen could get me.

Horrible big sister or not, this dog training thing isn't easy or quick. I get all uptight when I'm trying to get Ugly to heel better, he still does his little squirming thing, and then he'll end up under my feet or taking off after a bird. Maggie is so calm and quiet when she's training Ugly, even when he's being annoying.

20

I t's been a whole week since I've trained Ugly with
Maggie. When she's with me, I kind of know what
to do, but when she's not around it's a whole lot harder,
and I almost give up on Ugly. Sometimes, I look up at
our kitchen window from where I am in the backyard
and I see Grandpa or one of my parents watching to see
how I'm doing. And if that's not pressure enough, this
afternoon Mrs. Manchester stuck her head over our
fence and asked, "Is that dog cat-proof yet?"

● ● ●

Honestly, it's now been a week since I wrote that
last paragraph and a whole two weeks since training

began and he's still not remembering all his lessons. Ugly is sure taking his time with becoming what Mom calls "manageable." Two weeks should be enough. I'm running out of patience. And Ugly doesn't know it, but he's running out of time.

When I told Hugh and Milly at school about Mrs. Manchester expecting me to cat-proof Ugly, they tried to help me with ideas. But even I knew Hugh was dreaming when he gave his solution.

"You capture Mrs. Manchester's cat and every cat you can find in the neighborhood. Next, you put all the cats into one room with Ugly. Then, you leave it to the cats to straighten him out. Forever after, he'll be terrified of cats."

"It's an interesting idea," said Milly, grinning that big gap-toothed smile of hers, "but even if you managed to collect a room full of cats, I can see things going very wrong."

"You have to let your imagination run wild to get your best ideas," said Hugh.

"Believe me, Hughie," I said, "your imagination has definitely run wild."

"I haven't finished yet," said Hugh. "I'm going to bring something amazing for you to school tomorrow—something that will cat-proof Ugly."

The "something amazing" was a raggedy stuffed-toy cat. It had large glass eyes and a lot of white whiskers; it looked incredibly real.

"You can keep it," said Hugh. "It's been played with by my cousins, then handed on to my sisters, and then to me."

"What am I supposed to do with a stuffed cat?" I asked, holding it by the tail so its head hung down to the ground.

HUGH'S AMAZING "CAT-PROOFING" STUFFED TOY

"Use it to train Ugly. Put the cat on the grass and make Ugly sit and stay while you pat the cat."

"Interesting theory," said Milly.

It was interesting, all right. Ugly ran off with the stuffed cat and dismembered it under the house.

"Dismembered" was the word Grandpa used after he helped me pick up all the pieces of toy cat.

21

For a while now, I've done what Milly suggested and stuck my training list on the wall next to my bed. I could tell you by heart what it says. I've been doing everything I said I would. I'm up extra early. I do all the caring for Ugly. I train him twice a day. I listen carefully to what Maggie tells me, and I try it out with Ugly.

It's taken nearly three weeks, but as long as there is nothing to distract him, Ugly seems to be getting the hang of heeling when he's on the leash. He'll also sit, but he has a ways to go before he'll stay until

I call. He's also pretty hopeless at dropping or lying down. And there is one thing that really annoys me.

Maggie says I need to give Ugly more playtime breaks, but when I want to throw the ball for him, he just won't bring it back. I try to pull it out of his mouth, and he seems to think that's funny.

On top of that, the highlight for Ugly on our walks to the park is still trying to catch Mrs. Manchester's cat when we walk past her house. Even if Penelope isn't around, Ugly behaves like a bloodhound. With his nose pressed on the ground, sniffing out cat smells, he pulls me around in circles.

Anyway, I'm looking forward to Saturday. Hugh and Milly are coming over to help me train Ugly.

22

When Milly was dropped off at my place with Hugh, she had a shoulder bag with her.

"I've had a brain wave," she said, patting her bag. "Let's go to your room."

"Not another stuffed cat, is it?" I asked.

"This will work," she said. "I've tried it on our dog. It will make Ugly drop the ball for you and it should also stop him from chasing next door's cat."

"You'll be a millionaire if you're right," said Hugh.

Once the three of us were in my bedroom, Milly opened her bag. She pulled out three plastic water pistols. "They hose dogs with water to stop them from fighting," explained Milly. "And police use water cannons to break up riots. It makes sense that we can use water to train Ugly."

We started with ball throwing and fetching. When Ugly ran back with the ball, one of us would squirt him. He really did drop the ball. But that didn't work forever. After a while, Ugly lost interest in playing ball.

That's when we tried the water pistol technique to cat-proof him.

We chose to walk Ugly to the park when we knew Mrs. Manchester's cat was sunbathing in her favorite place—on her front brick fence. Sure enough, when Ugly saw Penelope, he started yapping, jiggling, and pulling on the leash. Immediately, the three of us squirted him. He stepped back and was quiet for a moment, but then he lunged forward again. I wasn't holding on tight enough, and this time Ugly managed to get closer to the cat, who was still sitting but was now also snarling. Once again, the three of us let loose with our water pistols, but Hugh misjudged and gave the cat a blast of water. She yowled so loudly that Mrs. Manchester hurried out her front door. All she could see was one half-drowned cat clawing her way up a gum tree.

"What have you done to my Penelope?" she yelled.

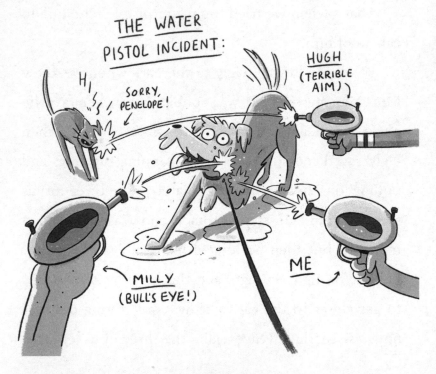

"We were trying to dog-proof her, Mrs. Manchester," I said.

"Go away! Just go away!" said Mrs. Manchester.

As we ran toward the park, Ugly trotted along, barking his head off. It sounded very much like laughing.

● ● ●

On Sunday, when Maggie visited, I told her about the water pistols.

Maggie shook her head in a disapproving way. "You can't carry water pistols around forever," she said. "Besides, you should stick to positive training methods. Use treats and rewards."

Then Maggie taught me this cool trick to get Ugly to bring his ball back. You pick up another one of his toys, which makes him forget he has the ball, so he comes back to you and drops it. Then, you pick up the ball and throw it again. Even playing with a dog needs owner training, it seems.

Maggie's way of training is pretty smart, but Ugly and I haven't got forever. I held the ball, and he looked up at me, grinning. I thought, *You wouldn't be grinning like that, poor dog, if you knew how serious the situation was.*

23

After a month of dog training (which feels as slow as a hundred years), Ugly has improved his behavior—but only when he feels like it. This afternoon, I took Ugly for a walk on the leash in the opposite direction from Mrs. Manchester and her cat. We must have walked about six doors down the street. All was fine until we came to a house where a small dog yapped at us from behind a high gate. Ugly charged across to the gate, barking and pulling me with him.

I was glad Maggie wasn't there because Ugly just ignored me. I tried to talk calmly, but I kind of lost it and I think I did a bit of human barking. I have to admit, the human barking didn't get me anywhere.

The two dogs were enjoying their hate session. The dog behind the fence was leaping around and jumping up at the gate. Ugly was doing the same thing on our side of the gate.

I've been wondering what I can do about a dog that only behaves himself at home. Will Maggie make us have the big test away from our place? Somewhere that has barking dogs? The only thing I can think to do is always make sure I have treats in my pocket—then I might be able to tempt Ugly into doing what I want.

24

I'm feeling a little better about training Ugly. The tough part has been sticking to all this for six weeks. Milly thinks that's how Olympic athletes must feel. She says there must be so many times when they want to give up day after day, but the difference between them and the rest of us ordinary people is that they just keep going.

Ugly seems to know the routine. I've started to give him fewer treats so that he doesn't always expect them, but I'm giving him just as much praise. It seems to work. Maggie calls it the "slot machine" method. Ugly only sometimes hits the "jackpot" (that means

getting a treat), but he's
always hoping for the
best, so he keeps on doing
what I ask—or most of
the time. That's what
makes me sort of on
edge. What if Ugly
messes up when it
comes time for Maggie
to decide if he's been
trained enough for me to
keep him?

25

I've been good with sticking to Ugly's feeding, walking, and training schedule. Hugh visited after school this week, and he says I'm way more patient. He's right. When I manage to forget that Ugly really has to pass his training, I enjoy teaching Ugly stuff.

After two long months, tomorrow is the big test. I've never in my whole life worked as hard as I have over the last few days. Last night, I was so tired I fell asleep during dinner. I just put my head down on the table for a moment and, next thing I remember, Dad was carrying me to bed like a little kid.

Every time I look at Ugly and he gives one of his

long, loving, brown-eyed looks, I just push myself onward. I've even added a training trick that Maggie hasn't told me about. I read about it on the internet. I want to surprise Maggie—show her how intelligent and obedient Ugly is.

Tonight has been the opposite from last night. At seven o'clock, Milly called me. "Hugh and I want you to know that we think you're an amazing dog trainer. Everyone in both our families wishes you the best of luck."

"Thanks, Milly," I said. "I know I've tried my very hardest, but one thing that worries me is if Ugly behaves badly."

"Just concentrate on being a team with Ugly," suggested Milly. "Try thinking like a dog."

After Milly's phone call, I

thought I'd go to bed early to get a good night's rest, but I haven't been able to sleep.

I know I should be thinking positive thoughts, but I keep imagining it all going wrong and having to say goodbye to Ugly.

About half an hour ago, I went into my parents' room to see if they were awake. Dad was sitting up in bed doing work on his computer. Mom was lying on her side, reading a book. They both looked up.

"Please just say I can keep Ugly," I said before they could ask why I was standing there. "I beg you." I thought about falling on my knees, but I know Dad isn't into that sort of thing.

"No need to be dramatic, Eccle," said Dad.

"Ugly is part of our family," I said.

Mom sat up and put her arms out to me. I walked over, and she hugged me.

"You love Ugly, Mom. How can you let this happen?"

Mom looked sadly at Dad. I wondered if she was

going to give in. But he shook his head at her. She took a deep breath and said, "I love Ugly and I want the best for him—and for you, Ec."

"But the best is just leaving everything like it is!" I said. I couldn't believe my parents could be so cruel.

"It's called tough love, Eccle," said Dad.

"We want you to grow up into the sort of man who knows how to work toward a goal—who knows that some of the best things don't come easily," said Mom.

"Someone who knows about responsibilities and that there are consequences for what we do or don't do," Dad added.

"But it's not fair to use poor Ugly to teach me to be a man," I said.

"Ugly also deserves to have an owner who can control him. He'll be a happier dog," said Dad.

I so much wanted to throw something. Boy, was I mad. But I knew that the "sort of man" Mom and Dad wanted me to be wouldn't throw things. Instead,

I yelled, "But don't you understand? Ugly is happier than ever. We...we like each other now."

"Well, tomorrow you can prove it," said Dad, and then he put out the light so that I had to feel my way to my bedroom.

Ugly was waiting for me in there. I put my arms around him and leaned my head into his hairy side.

"Don't worry, boy," I said, but those were just words. There was plenty to worry about, and Ugly knew it.

He licked my face and made snuffle sounds. I think he was saying, "I'm sad too. But cheer up. Together we might just make it."

26

Well, the big test day is over, but I still don't know if Ugly and I have passed. It's eight o'clock at night and I'm on my bed writing this. Ugly and I are exhausted. He's curled up next to me. Mom, Dad, Grandpa, and Maggie are in the kitchen making a final decision.

In my head, I've been going through the tests Ugly and I did with Maggie, trying to figure out what she'd be thinking now. There were definitely some wins, but there were also some bad moments. Maggie called them "unfortunate."

So I'm trying to make a list of the good and the

"unfortunate" things that happened today. First off, we had to walk to the park. But to get to the park, we had to pass Mrs. Manchester's house. Was that tease of a ginger cat going to be there? Please, no.

But she *was* there—sitting up on the brick fence as if she owned the world. The look on Penelope's face seemed to say, "I bet you, Ugly, that you won't be able to control yourself when you see me here!"

Sure enough, I could feel Ugly tense up on the leash. It would just be a couple of seconds before he'd rip free and take off. Maggie and I hadn't done any chasing cat lessons, and I couldn't count on Milly's water pistol method, so I had to think for myself. I swung around to face Ugly so that I was between him and the cat. I gently pulled his leash upward and at the same time lifted my hand above Ugly's nose, as if I was going to rest a treat there.

"Sit!" I said in a firm voice. I didn't think he'd obey, but Ugly slowly sat down, the way dogs do when they really don't want to. I slipped him a small treat, patted him, and told him he was good. Then I quickly looked over my shoulder.

The cat was still sitting there, and I'm sure I saw a curtain in Mrs. Manchester's front window lift and fall. She was spying. I wasn't going to let that woman and her smarty-pants cat wreck Ugly's chances right at the start of his test. We couldn't stand there forever waiting for the cat to move, but if we walked past her, I knew I'd lose control of Ugly.

The only thing left to do was to not walk past Mrs. Manchester's house. But we couldn't retreat and go back home; that would be failing too. We still had to get to the park. I gave a quick tug on Ugly's leash and said, "Walk!"

I moved in a new direction so that Ugly was walking away from the cat and toward the edge of the road, where I made him sit again. Then we crossed the road. We walked along the sidewalk on the other side of the road, past two houses. Then I walked to the edge of the road and made Ugly sit again, and we crossed back again so we arrived just where the park was. Maggie was following, but she didn't say anything.

What happened in the park might also be a mixture of good and unfortunate. I'm waiting to hear what Maggie will say about it. Maggie was asking me to make Ugly sit, stay, and come. He was doing it okay, but Mrs. Manchester suddenly arrived. She was holding a little boy's hand. He looked about four years old. He climbed onto a swing and Mrs. Manchester started to push him. Ugly rushed across to play with the boy. The boy laughed happily as Ugly showed off by running around in little circles. I walked across and held on to Ugly so that the boy could pat him.

"This is my grandson, Jack," said Mrs. Manchester.

"Hello, Jack," I said. "This is my dog—Ugly."

"He's not ugly," said Jack. "He's booful."

"I think he's beautiful too," I said.

Ugly wagged his tail and gave a happy yap.

After that, I led Ugly to a quiet corner of the park where we could continue with his obedience testing. I could see Mrs. Manchester had finished pushing Jack on the swing. She was now helping him up the ladder to the slide. At the same moment, a tall man with a hoodie pulled so far down over his face that you couldn't see his eyes came running across the park. It looked like he was heading for Mrs. Manchester. Maggie and I stopped and looked to see what the man wanted.

What happened next was a shock. The man ran right up to Mrs. Manchester, who had her back to him, and grabbed the strap of her handbag, which was over her shoulder. Mrs. Manchester lost her balance and nearly fell.

"No!" she yelled, and Jack started crying loudly.

Everything after that happened before you could count to three. I was staring, frozen. Even Maggie was frozen. But Ugly wasn't. He was tearing across the grass toward the handbag thief. He was jumping and dancing in circles around the man. The man tried to kick Ugly. I called Ugly, and he dived past the man again and tried to run back to me. In the same moment, the man tripped over Ugly and went sprawling. Mrs. Manchester's handbag flew across the grass. By then, Maggie and I were running to help Mrs. Manchester and Jack.

The man yelled some incredibly rude words at Ugly. He pulled himself up and limped, staggered, and jogged out of sight.

Maggie was looking after Mrs. Manchester and young Jack. I checked on poor Ugly. He came up to me with his tail between his legs. He didn't like getting shouted at by the man, but he probably also felt guilty about running away from his obedience test. Just the same, I patted him and said, "Good dog. You saved Mrs. Manchester's handbag."

Although his tail stayed low, it started wagging a

tiny bit. It was like he was saying, "Please don't be mad at me. I was only doing my best."

"Your dog saved my handbag," said Mrs. Manchester, holding her grandson to her like she'd never let him go. "I couldn't care less about any money being stolen. It's the baby photos in there of young Jack with my dear husband who died three years back. They're precious. I was going to get extra prints made. Ugly is a brave and intelligent dog—even if he *does* give my cat a little too much attention."

I think Ugly is brave and intelligent too, but what do Maggie and the rest of my family think? They're all in the kitchen, talking about Ugly. This pen keeps dropping out of my hand. I have to jerk myself awake. I'll just rest my head for a few minutes and then I'll start writing again when I'm fresher.

27

THE ENDING

I'm over the moon. Last night was wonderful. I had fallen asleep with this book on my chest. Dad woke me up with the news that Maggie and my family also think Ugly is a good, brave dog! Maggie says I've done "some solid work" with Ugly. As long as I continue with dog training classes, Maggie knows Ugly will be in good hands. Ugly is here to stay!

I've already started planning what Ugly and I are going to do together. And now that I've almost finished writing this book, I've decided to write another book.

It will be about training and looking after dogs. I'll be writing it for kids like me. It will have sections on things like:

- how to stop a dog chasing a cat
- what to do if your dog poops under or on your bed
- how to stop a dog chewing your school projects and precious possessions
- how to stop a puppy from biting your toes
- games dogs like to play
- why your dog stares at you
- how to tell if your dog is hypnotizing you and what to do about it
- ten smelly, yummy dog treat recipes
- how to stop a dog from eating other dogs' poop
- how to stop a dog from eating your socks or running off with your sister's tights

- what to feed a dog so it doesn't have stinky farts
- twelve reasons dogs have bad breath
- how to read your dog's future by its paw
- tips on how to stick to training even when you don't seem to be getting anywhere
- dog psychology—how to tell if your dog is lonely, sad, embarrassed, jealous, angry, or bored
- useful and unusual tricks to teach your dog

This afternoon we had a graduation ceremony for Ugly. We had a big crowd. All of our family of Brights was there—Mom, Dad, Grandpa, Gretchen, and Gretchen's boyfriend, Shane. My school friends, Milly (with a red ribbon around her ponytail) and Hugh, who had made a big poster that said, CONGRATULATIONS ECCLE AND UGLY!, were there too. Mrs. Manchester was also there (without Penelope), and she had her grandson, Jack, and his mother, Nina, with her. Of course, Maggie, who had spent so much time helping me learn how to train Ugly, was there, as well.

The party was in the back garden. Hugh, Milly, and I decorated Ugly's doghouse with flowers. We also made Ugly a necklace of flowers, but he shook it off. I gave Ugly a new chewy toy—a rubber chicken that squeaks. He likes it a lot. Maggie made Ugly sit and then she presented him and me with a graduation certificate:

DOG TRAINING GRADUATION CERTIFICATE

Ugly Bright

HIGH DISTINCTION

Something really amazing happened next. Jack's mom, Nina, stepped forward.

"The Manchester family have something to give Ugly too. This dog saved my mother-in-law's handbag and the photos inside. We're giving Ugly a year's supply of dog treats and this medal."

Nina handed me a ginormous plastic bag full of packets of dog treats. Next, she held out a golden dog tag. It looked just like a small Olympic medal. We all took a look. These words were on it:

UGLY
DOG HERO

The medal had a tiny hole at the top so that I could hang it on his collar. Ugly sat quietly while I attached it. When I had finished, he leaped around yapping. His tail was spinning in happy circles. Everyone clapped and laughed. Ugly barked even more. He grinned and rushed around, getting pats. His medal sparkled in the sun.

Now it was time for Ugly to amaze everyone with the trick I've been secretly teaching him.

I held up my hand. "Sit!" I said to Ugly. He sat down, and I gave him a treat.

"Look at me!" I said. Ugly's ears pricked up and his bright eyes peered through his bangs into mine.

"Hello, Ugly!" I said, spreading my hand out like a star in front of Ugly's face.

UGLY'S GRADUATION!

CONGRATULATIONS ECCLE + UGLY!

"Huuwoo!" said Ugly, and he grinned. "Huuwoo!" he said again.

The cheering was deafening. Ugly woofed and woofed and thumped his tail on the ground. I crouched down beside him, and he gave my face a slobbery lick. "Ewww," I said, laughing and wiping away the dog slobber. I thought about the amazing things that had happened in my life and in Ugly's life. I wrapped my arms around Ugly and pressed my face into my friend's big furry chest. At the same moment, I thought, *Of course, my dog still doesn't like me—instead, he loves me, and I love him!*

Acknowledgments

Eric thanks Meg H. for generously sharing her expert knowledge about dogs and their responsible care. He apologizes if he has in any way misconstrued her advice, and he assures her that he will continue to work assiduously on his dog handling skills.

Elizabeth Fensham is very grateful to the UQP team—Kristina Schultz, Michele Perry, and Karin Cox—for their helpful insights and guidance. She thanks her husband, Robert, for his warmhearted and practical support. Her appreciation is also extended to Timothy and Alison Fensham for valued insights.

Finally, big hugs and heartfelt thanks to all the children who helped Eric with his research. Your ideas were hilarious and brilliant.

About the Author

Elizabeth Fensham lives in Victoria's Dandenong Ranges. She is married to an artist and has two adult sons. Fensham has been writing in earnest for the last twenty years. Her first novel, *The Helicopter Man*, won the Children's Book Council of Australia (CBCA) Book of the Year for Younger Readers in 2006. Previous young adult novels include *Miss McAllister's Ghost* and *Goodbye Jamie Boyd*, which was shortlisted for the Bologna Book Fair's White Ravens Award in 2009. Elizabeth's younger reader novel, *Matty Forever*, was shortlisted for the CBCA Book of the Year for Younger Readers in 2009. The companion, *Bill Rules*, was published in 2010. Her most recent young adult book is the moving *The Invisible Hero*, which won the Speech Pathology Australia Book of the Year Award in 2012 and is listed as an International Board on Books for Young People (IBBY) book.